by Jayneen Sanders   illustrated by Courtney Dawson

ABC

OF
BODY
SAFETY
AND CONSENT

a book to teach children about body safety, consent, safe and
unsafe touch, private parts, body boundaries and respect

TO MY WONDERFUL PARTNER IN LIFE AND IN WORK WHO ENCOURAGED ME TO WRITE THIS BOOK

J.S.

ABC of Body Safety and Consent
Educate2Empower Publishing an imprint of
UpLoad Publishing Pty Ltd
Victoria Australia
www.upload.com.au

First published in 2020
Reprinted in 2023

Written by Jayneen Sanders
Illustrations by Courtney Dawson

Jayneen Sanders asserts her right to be identified as the author of this work.

Courtney Dawson asserts her right to be identified as the illustrator of this work.

Designed by Stephanie Spartels, Studio Spartels

ISBN: 9781925089592 (hbk) 9781925089585 (pbk)

A catalogue record for this book is available from the National Library of Australia

Disclaimer: The information in this book is advice only written by the author based on her advocacy in this area, and her experience working with children as a classroom teacher and mother. The information is not meant to be a substitute for professional advice. If you are concerned about a child's behavior seek professional help.

NOTE TO THE READER

This book has been designed to be read at a conversational pace. It is best read with your child over a number of sittings and to revisit the information often; dipping in and out, and not necessarily in sequential order. The child-centered questions on each page are written to engage children in the discussions and reinforce the learning. There are Discussion Questions on pages 36–39 to help adults unpack these important skills with children.

The 26 key letters and accompanying words in this book will help your child retain crucial and life-changing body safety and consent information. The general Body Safety Rules below are a summary of what your child will learn as you guide them through this book.

1. MY BODY IS MY BODY

My body is my body and it belongs to me. I can say 'No!' if I don't want to kiss or hug someone. I can give them a hi-five or shake their hand.

2. SAFETY NETWORK

I have a Safety Network. These are 3 to 5 adults who I trust. I can tell these people anything and they will believe me. If I feel worried, scared or uncomfortable, I can tell someone on my Safety Network how I am feeling and why I feel this way.

3. EARLY WARNING SIGNS

If I feel frightened or unsafe, I might get a sick tummy or my heart might beat really fast. These feelings are called my Early Warning Signs. If I feel this way about anything, I need to tell an adult on my Safety Network straightaway.

4. PRIVATE PARTS

I always call my private parts by their correct names. No one can touch my private parts. No one can show me their private parts or ask me to touch their private parts, and no one should show me pictures of private parts. If any of these things happen, I need to tell a trusted adult on my Safety Network straightaway.

5. NO SECRETS

I don't keep secrets — only happy surprises that will be told. If someone asks me to keep a secret, I tell them I don't keep secrets. If someone asks me to keep a secret that makes me feel unsafe, I need to tell adult an on my Safety Network straightaway.

Note: a child-friendly 'My Body Safety Rules' poster is free to download from www.e2epublishing.info

A IS FOR ALWAYS

tell a trusted adult if you feel worried, scared or unsafe.

Have you ever felt unsafe?
What makes you feel unsafe?

B IS FOR BODY BOUNDARY.

This is the invisible space around your body that is just for you. No one can come inside your body boundary without your *consent.

*Go to page 6 to explore the meaning of consent.

Should a doctor or dentist ask for your consent before they come inside your body boundary?

C IS FOR CONSENT.

Consent means you have said 'Yes' to someone coming inside your body boundary and you have HAPPILY agreed to this.

When might you give your consent (happily say 'Yes') to someone?

D IS FOR DON'T

be afraid to tell a trusted adult if you feel unsafe or someone has asked you to keep an unsafe secret. Remember, trusted adults are there to help you.

What might an unsafe secret be?

E IS FOR EARLY WARNING SIGNS.

These are the feelings we get in our body when we feel unsafe.
You might get a sick tummy, shaky legs, your heart might beat
really fast and you might want to go to the toilet. You might
get only one of these Early Warning Signs or lots of them.
But you should tell a trusted adult as soon as you do.

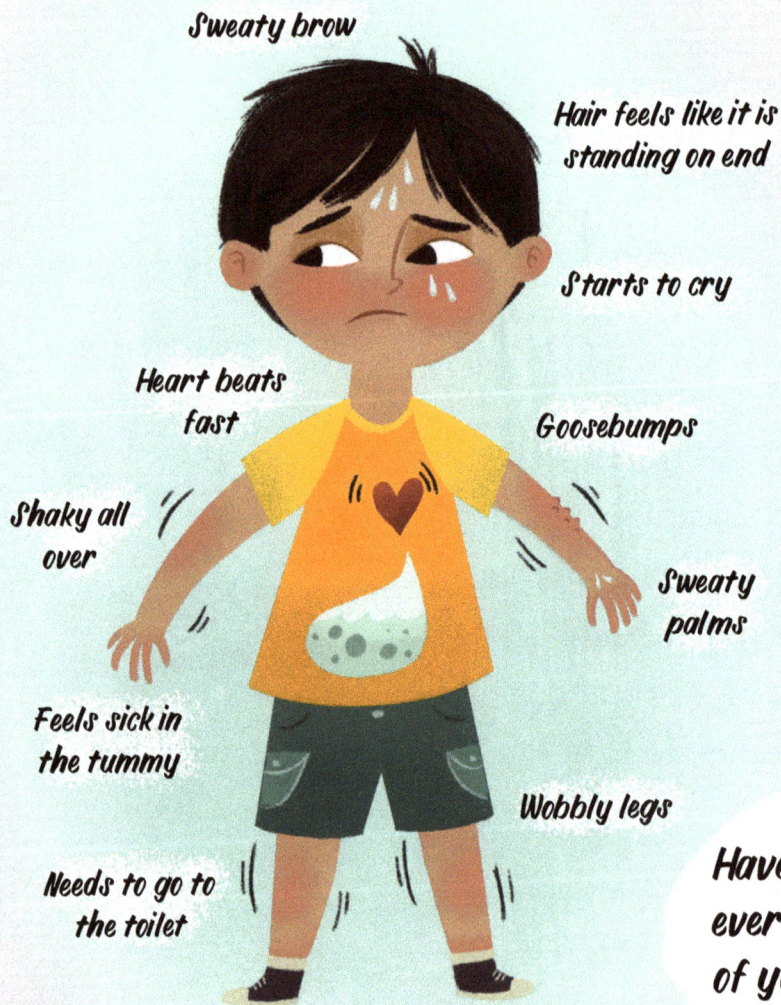

Sweaty brow

Hair feels like it is
standing on end

Starts to cry

Heart beats
fast

Goosebumps

Shaky all
over

Sweaty
palms

Feels sick in
the tummy

Wobbly legs

Needs to go to
the toilet

*Have you
ever felt any
of your Early
Warning Signs?*

E IS ALSO FOR EQUALITY.

Equality means everyone should be treated the same no matter who they are, where they come from, if they have a disability or not, or if they are a girl or a boy. We are all equal, and we should all be shown kindness and respect.

How are you the same as your friend? How are you different?

F IS FOR FEELINGS.

We all have feelings. You have feelings and your friends have feelings. You might feel happy in the morning but sad in the afternoon. Our feelings are always changing.

worried

proud

calm

happy

sad

brave

angry

scared

disappointed

confused

lonely

shame

guilty

embarrassed

excited

Which feelings might you have when you feel safe? Which feelings might you have when you feel unsafe?

G IS FOR GO

straightaway to a trusted adult if you ever feel unsafe.

If that adult does not have time to listen, GO to another trusted adult who will listen to you.

Who are the adults you could go to if you felt unsafe?

H IS FOR HI-FIVES OR HANDSHAKES.

If you don't want to hug or kiss someone when saying 'Hello', you can choose to give them a hi-five, a handshake or blow them a kiss; even if they are an adult. You are the boss of your body and the choice is always yours.

How do you like to say 'Hello'? Is the way you greet people always the same?

I IS FOR NEVER IGNORE

your Early Warning Signs. If you feel any of them at anytime, tell a trusted adult straightaway.

What might some of your Early Warning Signs be?

J IS FOR JOKES

that are NOT funny about other people, especially about their private parts. If anyone tells you jokes about private parts or shows you pictures of private parts, tell a trusted adult straightaway.

What should you do if someone tries to tell you jokes about private parts?

K IS FOR KINDNESS

shown to people, especially if they are scared, hurt or feeling sad. It is good to be kind to other people. It is also good to be kind to yourself.

How do you show kindness to other people and to yourself? Who shows kindness to you? How do they do this?

L IS FOR LISTEN

to your body if you feel unsafe. Your body is very clever; it lets you know when it feels unsafe. Always tell a trusted adult if your body's Early Warning Signs begin.

What does it mean to listen to your body? What are your Early Warning Signs?

M IS FOR MY SAFETY NETWORK.

Your Safety Network is made up of 3 to 5 adults that you trust. These are the people that if you told them anything that made you feel worried or unsafe, they would listen to you and always believe you. One of the adults on your Safety Network should not be a family member.

Grandma

Mr Ross

Mama

Dad

My Safety Network

Grandma

Dad

Mama

Mr Ross
(my teacher)

Who are the trusted adults
on your Safety Network?

N IS FOR NO!

It's okay to say 'No' if an adult or a child comes inside your body boundary.

It's okay to say 'No' if an adult or a child asks to see or touch your private parts.

It's okay to say 'No' if an adult or a child wants you to look at or touch their private parts.

And it's okay to say 'No' if an adult or a child shows you pictures or videos of private parts.

If any of these things happen, run away quickly and tell someone on your Safety Network straightaway. Remember to keep on telling until you are believed. If you feel frightened or scared and you can't say 'No', never feel bad or blame yourself — just get away as quickly as you can and tell someone on your Safety Network straightaway.

O IS FOR OPEN CONVERSATIONS.

This means you can talk to a trusted adult about anything that is worrying you or you are curious about.

What are you curious about?

P IS FOR PRIVATE PARTS.

Private means just for you. Your private parts are the parts of your body under your bathing suit or underwear. Boys usually have a penis, testicles and a bottom. Girls usually have a vulva on the outside and a vagina on the inside. They also have nipples and a bottom. When girls get older, the area around their nipples grow into breasts. People sometimes call our private parts silly names like 'pee pee' or 'fanny'. But we should always use the correct names for our private parts. If anyone touches your private parts, you must tell a trusted adult on your Safety Network straightaway. Your mouth is a private part too.

P IS ALSO FOR PRIVATE AND PUBLIC PLACES.

Private means just for you but public means people share the space. Your bedroom is a private place, but the kitchen is a public place.

Can you think of some other private and public places?

Q IS FOR QUICKLY

run away from a person who makes you feel unsafe and tell a trusted adult on your Safety Network straightaway.

What is something (or someone) that might make you feel unsafe?

R IS FOR RESPECT.

We need to respect other people's body boundaries. Just as you may not like people coming inside your body boundary, you have to respect other people's wishes too. That means if you want to hug or kiss someone and they say 'No', then you have to respect their 'No'.

What do you think 'respect' means?

$\mathcal{S}$ IS FOR SECRETS

that make you feel unsafe or uncomfortable. If someone asks you to keep a secret that makes you feel this way, never ever keep that kind of secret.
Tell a trusted adult on your Safety Network straightaway.

S IS ALSO FOR SURPRISES.

Surprises will always be told. If someone asks you to keep a secret, tell that person you don't keep secrets. You only keep 'happy surprises' because surprises will always be told.

What do you think is the difference between 'secrets' and 'surprises'?

T IS FOR TELL

a trusted adult on your Safety Network if you ever feel unsafe or your Early Warning Signs begin.

Who are the people on your Safety Network?

U IS FOR UNSAFE FEELINGS.

You might feel scared, worried, sad or angry. If you have any of these unsafe feelings, always tell a trusted adult on your Safety Network.

Have you ever felt unsafe? How did it make you feel?

V IS FOR VERY BRAVE.

Remember, it is very brave to tell a trusted adult that you feel unsafe, or that someone has touched your private parts or shown you pictures of private parts.
It's hard to be brave, especially if an older person has told you not to tell — but remember, you are braver than you think and telling a trusted adult is very important.

If someone touched your private parts and told you not to tell anyone, what would you do?

W IS FOR WARNING WORD.

Every family needs a family warning word. This is a word that only family members know. For example, if you are away from home and you ring up and say 'carrots' (because that is your family warning word) your family member knows to come and get you straightaway because you are feeling unsafe.

What is your family warning word?

X IS FOR BLOWING XXXXX (KISSES)

to greet people you know well because you may not feel like giving them a hug or a kiss.

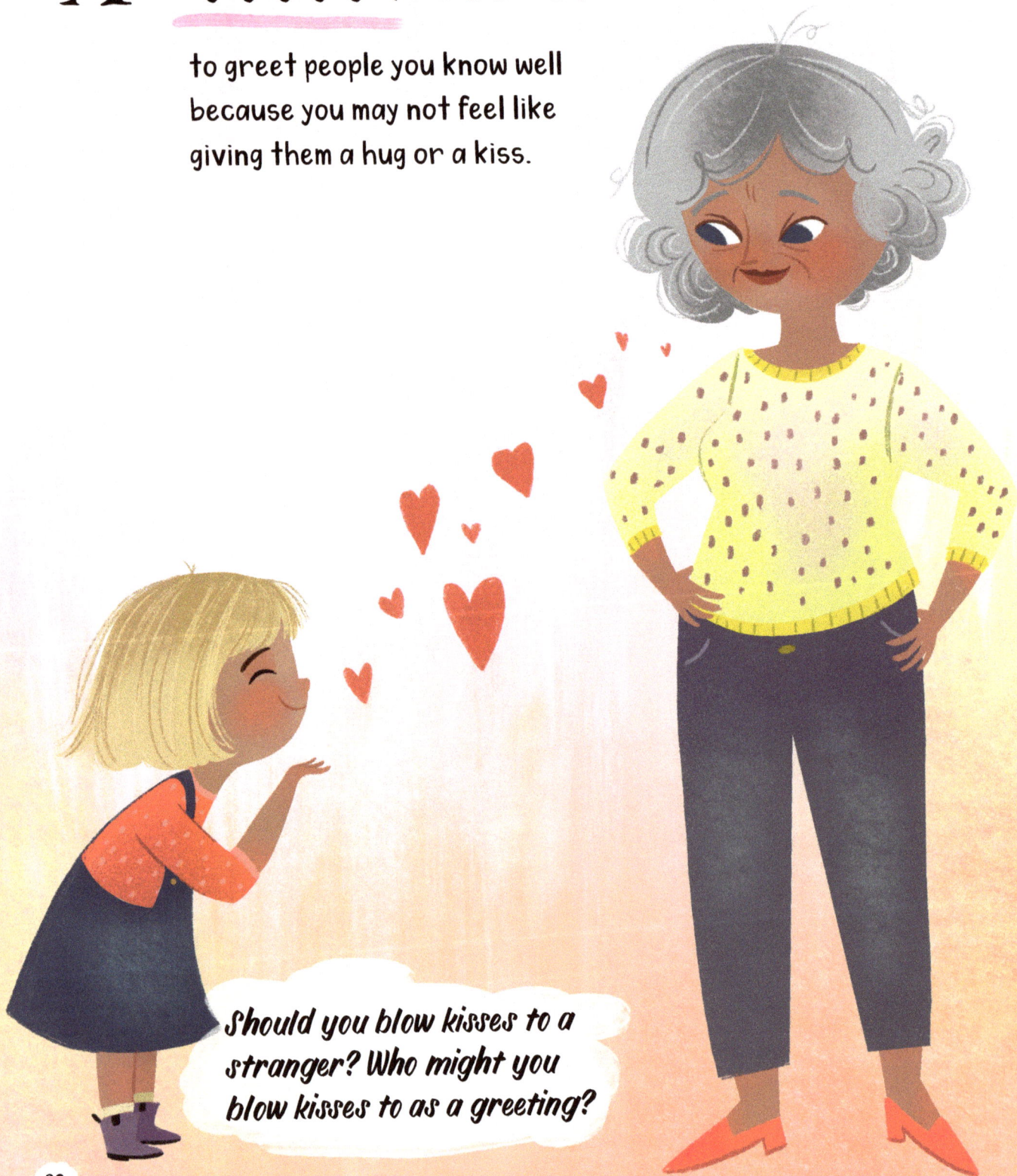

Should you blow kisses to a stranger? Who might you blow kisses to as a greeting?

Y IS FOR YES.

If you want to give a friend or a family member a kiss or a hug you can say 'Yes' when they ask you. This means you have happily given your consent.

What does 'consent' mean?

Z IS FOR ZOOM

away quickly from anyone or anything that makes you feel unsafe, and tell a trusted adult on your Safety Network straightaway.

What will you always do if you feel unsafe?

AND ALWAYS REMEMBER, YOU ARE THE **BOSS OF YOUR BODY** AND **WHAT YOU SAY GOES!**

DISCUSSION QUESTIONS FOR PARENTS, CAREGIVERS AND EDUCATORS

The following Discussion Questions are intended as a guide, and can be used to initiate an open and empowering dialogue with your child around body safety, body boundaries, consent, respect, feelings and emotions, secrets and surprises, and recognizing unsafe situations. These questions/discussion points are optional and can be explored at different readings. However, they will assist you and your child to unpack this important topic and to explore the skills outlined within the book.

Each letter can be used as a 'key' to recalling a body safety skill, for example, you could ask, 'Do you remember what "S" stands for?' In this way, each key letter will assist the child to memorize the skill the letter links to. You could also make your own posters for each letter by either scribing what your child says or have them write down their summary of the skill on poster paper. They could then add their own illustrations to further reinforce the learning. These posters could be displayed for all to see, including visitors, and stimulate more discussion around this topic with other adults and children. Finally, as you and your child read the text at various sittings, discuss both the questions and the illustrations, and encourage your child to offer their ideas and opinions. This book has been designed specifically to be a 'dip in and dip out' book, and to both teach and reinforce Body Safety skills.

Note: before pages 18 to 19 where a Safety Network is discussed, the term 'trusted adult' has been used. This 'trusted adult' will become part of your child's Safety Network.

Page 4: A is for ALWAYS ...

Talk about times when your child felt unsafe. Ask, 'What should you do if you feel unsafe?' Discuss the meaning of 'trusted adult'.

Page 5: B is for BODY BOUNDARY

Discuss with your child what a body boundary (aka body bubble) is. Have you and your child outline your body boundaries. Talk about what 'consent' means and when it needs to be asked for. Ask, 'Can anyone come inside your body boundary without your consent?' Discuss. Say, 'If someone comes inside your body boundary you have the right to say "No" and to place your hand out in front of you.'

Page 6: C is for CONSENT

Discuss what 'consent' means, especially in regard to coming inside a person's body boundary. Talk about the ways people can say 'Yes', for example, 'For sure', 'Absolutely okay' and 'You can'. Discuss how people may give their consent but their body language is saying 'No' as they might be frightened to say 'No' to someone, especially an adult. Reinforce that giving your consent means you have **happily** said 'Yes' and your body language reflects that also. Point out that you must always ask for consent too, such as asking a person for a hug rather than just 'taking' it. Discuss how you might share these ideas with extended family members and friends.

Page 7: D is DON'T ...

Discuss with your child the idea that sometimes we have to be brave even though we may not feel very brave at all. Reiterate that if they feel unsafe or someone tells them an unsafe secret that it is very important to tell a trusted adult. Identify who their trusted adults might be. Ask, 'If that adult does not have time to listen to you or doesn't understand, what should you do?' The answer is to tell another trusted adult and keep on telling until they are listened to and believed.

Page 8: E is for EARLY WARNING SIGNS

Discuss how everyone has Early Warning Signs when they feel unsafe, and that our bodies are incredibly smart and let us know when we feel unsafe. Ask, 'What does your body do if you feel unsafe?' Discuss. Talk about what your child needs to do if their Early Warning Signs kick in. Remind children that sometimes, if they are 'risking on purpose' such as climbing up a rock wall, they might also get some of these feelings but these feelings are to do with excitement and challenges rather than feeling unsafe.

Page 9: E is also for EQUALITY

Talk about the meaning of 'equality' in terms of race, gender and ability. Ask, 'What does "kindness" mean? What does "respect" mean?' Ask your child to provide examples of kindness and/or respect shown to them or when they saw this behavior in a book or on TV. *Note:* most often children do not see difference; it's usually the adults around them that reinforce stereotyping. Ensure your child knows everyone matters, no matter who they are or where they come from, and that even though we are all more the same than we are different, it is our individual differences that make us unique.

Pages 10–11: F is for FEELINGS

Talk about the boy's facial expressions and the 'feeling' words underneath. Pick two or three 'feeling' words and ask, 'When have you felt ...?' Take your time to explore this page with your child; there are many expressions to take in. The idea is for your child to increase their 'feelings' vocabulary so they have the words to express how they are feeling as they grow. Let your child know it's important for them to express how they are feeling (especially when they feel unsafe) to you or a trusted adult. Discuss how our feelings are always changing — it might be because of a situation, another person or we may not know why we are feeling a certain way. Reassure your child that our changing feelings are normal and natural, but if a feeling makes us unhappy, sad or anxious (negative feelings) we need to tell a trusted adult. *Note:* see the book 'Talking About Feelings' by Jayneen Sanders for more on this topic.

Page 12: G is for GO ...

Ensure your child knows to GO to a trusted adult as soon as they feel unsafe. Reinforce that if that adult is not available or is too busy or does not understand, to go to another trusted adult on their Safety Network (see pages 18 and 19), and if that person is unavailable, to keep telling until they are listened to and believed.

Page 13: H is for HI-FIVES or HANDSHAKES

Ask, 'What does, "You are the boss of your body" mean?' Review body boundaries (page 5) and consent (page 6). Lead into a discussion about how your child might like to greet people. Reinforce that it's always their choice. If they wish to give a hug and/or a kiss as a greeting, they can. If they wish to give a hi-five, handshake or blow a kiss to someone they know well, then this is their choice. Talk about how people should ask them for a kiss or a hug, and they have the right to say 'Yes' or 'No'. *Note:* I often say that parents may be given a 'free pass' for hugs and kisses but only if the child has willingly given their consent to this idea. Never be insulted if, from time to time, your child doesn't want a kiss or a hug. Just like adults, children sometimes like their personal space, and that's okay.

Page 14: I is for never IGNORE ...

Review your child's Early Warning Signs (see page 8). You could draw a body shape outline on some paper and have them write labels pertaining to their own Early Warning Signs, for example, heart beating fast, shaky legs, etc.

Page 15: J is for JOKES ...

We want our kids to grow into 'upstanders' — meaning they call out people over bullying behaviors and/or jokes about private parts, but only if it is safe to do so. Reinforce that if your child hears jokes or sees pictures of private parts or unsafe content, they need to tell a trusted adult straightaway.

Page 16: K is for KINDNESS ...

Discuss what kindness, compassion and empathy mean. Read the text and questions with your child and discuss. *Note:* for a more in-depth exploration of this topic see 'You, Me and Empathy' written by Jayneen Sanders.

Page 17: L is for LISTEN

Read the text and examine the illustration with your child. Ask, 'What Early Warning Signs do you think these children are feeling? How would you feel if you were with these children? What might your Early Warning Signs be? What other ways do you listen to your body?'

Pages 18–19: M is for MY SAFETY NETWORK

On a piece of paper outline your (or your child's) hand. On each finger have them (or you) write the 3 to 5 adults on their Safety Network. These will be adults who they trust, who they are comfortable to tell anything to, who will listen to and believe them, and who are available to your child. One should not be a family member. The adults they put on their Safety Network must be your child's choice. *Note:* the choice may surprise you. The person who you think they might want on there may not (for whatever reason) be the person they choose. But it **is** the child's choice. Reinforce to your child that the people they choose to be on their Safety Network are their trusted adults. *Note:* discuss the different names your child might use for these people so everyone is on the same page.

Page 20: N is for NO!

Read through the text with your child. Take your time to discuss each scenario. Reassure your child that they have the right to say 'No' even to an adult or older child if they feel unsafe. *Note:* just like adults, children may and do 'freeze' when it comes to saying 'No' to unsafe touch and/or uncomfortable situations. Therefore: 1. Have your child practice standing in a superhero pose (like the girl in the illustration) and place their hand out and say 'No'. 2. You could say, 'If you find it difficult to say "No" for any reason, make sure you go to a trusted adult on your Safety Network straightaway.' Of course, we want to empower children so we don't really want them to think this is an option; but if in reality they are in an unsafe situation and they do 'freeze', we don't want them to blame themselves either. Practicing saying 'No' is very important and it's also very empowering.

Page 21: O is for OPEN CONVERSATIONS

Ensure your child knows that they can talk to you about anything. Explain that an 'open conversation' means they can ask you about anything that is worrying them or they are curious about. Make sure they know you are always there to listen to them and that they should never feel afraid, worried or ashamed to ask questions. Try starting some open conversations, for example, in the car on the way to school.

Page 22: P is for PRIVATE PARTS

Read through the text with your child and discuss. Discuss the word 'private' as meaning 'just for you'. If you wish to show your child appropriate drawings of private parts to discuss the difference between boys and girls anatomically, you can download free, age-appropriate line drawings of children's private parts at www.e2epublishing.info under Free Resources. Discuss why the mouth is a private part, and that even though we see a boy's nipples when he is in his bathing suit or underwear, these are private also. Explain that just as we use the correct names for our elbows or toes, we use the correct names for our private parts. For reasons why we encourage children and adults to use the correct names for their private parts go to the blog '8 Reasons NOT to Call Your Child's Genitals "Pet" Names' at www.e2epublishing.info/blog

Page 23: P is for also for PRIVATE AND PUBLIC PLACES

Help children to understand the difference between a private place/space and a public place/space. It is important that children understand that the bathroom, toilet and bedroom are private places and people need to ask permission before coming in. Relate back to the previous page where 'private' means 'just for you'. We want children to be comfortable and not ashamed of their private parts so they need to know it's okay for them to touch their own private parts (which can feel good) but only in a private space.

Page 24: Q is for QUICKLY ...

Review with your child what they should do if they feel unsafe.

Page 25: R is for RESPECT

Talk about what respect means in general and also in terms of body boundaries. Ensure your child knows that people need to show respect for their body boundary, decisions, preferences, feelings and wishes; just as they should respect other people's.

Pages 26–27: S is for SECRETS; S is also for SURPRISES

Read these two pages together. 'Secrets', in reality, is a word that society continues to use. However, encourage your family or class to use the word 'surprises' instead as surprises will always be told. Ask, 'What should you do if you are told an unsafe secret and/or a secret that makes you feel uncomfortable and/or a secret that switches on your Early Warning Signs? What might be some examples of happy surprises?'

Page 28: T is for TELL …

Review the importance of telling a trusted adult if your child feels unsafe or their Early Warning Signs begin. Go over the names of the people on your child's Safety Network.

Page 29: U is for UNSAFE FEELINGS

Review unsafe feelings and also feelings where your child might feel angry or anxious. Remind them when they feel this way to tell a trusted adult. When a child is angry they may wish to hit out, so it's important to also let them know they can talk about angry feelings too, before those feelings lead to unsafe behaviors. Notice and praise your child for their courage and bravery. Explain that saying 'No' to someone older is a difficult thing to do but sometimes they have to be very brave. However, also explain that they are a child, and if it's difficult to say 'No' you will always understand, and that they should never feel guilty for not being able to say 'No'. However, (the main point here) they must tell a trusted adult on their Safety Network what has happened, and keep on telling until they are believed.

Page 31: W is for WARNING WORD

Read the text and then ask, 'What should our family warning word be? Why do you think we need a family warning word? Who should we tell the family warning word to?' Note: a family warning word is ideal for older children going alone (or without any family members) to parties and sleepovers.

Page 32: X is for blowing XXXXX (KISSES) …

Ask, 'How might you greet people you know well? Do you always have to kiss or hug them? Should you greet a stranger by blowing them kisses? Why do you say that?' Explain that blowing kisses is an ideal way to greet someone you know well or love, especially when you don't want them coming inside your body boundary at this particular greeting. Remind your child that next time you may wish to give them a kiss on the cheek or a hug, but each greeting can be different; and that's okay. Note: you may need to remind some adults of this point as well.

Page 33: Y is for YES

Explain to your child that 'Yes' is a wonderful word when you have **happily** given your consent (see page 6 for more on consent). Just as we explain to children that they can say 'No', the upside is they can also say 'Yes'. It is always **their** choice. Remind your child that consent is about choice — people need to ask them for a hug or a kiss and they have a choice, for example, they can say, 'No, thanks' and give a hi-five as a greeting or they can say 'Yes' and have a big happy hug. But it is always **their** choice!

Page 34: Z is for ZOOM

Revisit what your child should do if they feel unsafe.

Page 35

Ask, 'Who is the boss of your body?' Encourage the shouting out of 'Me!' Have your child stand in a superhero pose and say in a loud, clear and empowered voice, 'I am the boss of my body! And what I say goes!'

BOOKS BY THE SAME AUTHOR

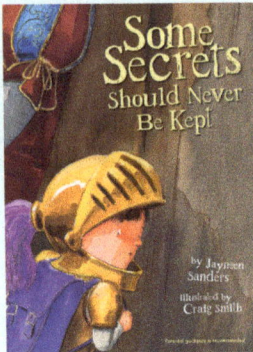

Some Secrets Should Never Be Kept

This book sensitively raises the subject of safe and unsafe touch, and assists caregivers and educators to broach this subject with children in a non-threatening and age-appropriate way. Discussion Questions included. Ages 3 to 11 years.

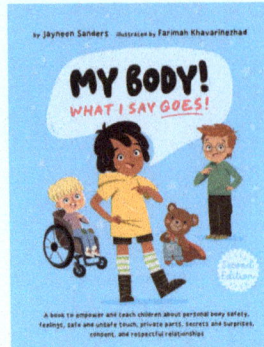

My Body! What I Say Goes!

A children's picture book to empower and teach children about personal body safety, feelings, safe and unsafe touch, private parts, secrets and surprises, consent and respect. Discussion Questions included. Ages 3 to 9 years.

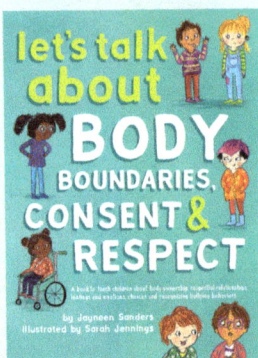

Let's Talk About Body Boundaries, Consent & Respect

Through familiar scenarios, this book opens up crucial conversations with children around body boundaries, consent and respect. Discussion Questions included. Ages 4 to 10 years.

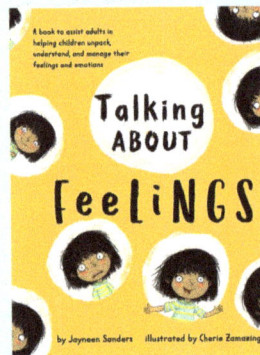

Talking About Feelings

A book to assist adults in helping children to unpack, understand, and manage their feelings and emotions in an engaging and interactive way. Discussion Questions included. Ages 4 to 10 years.

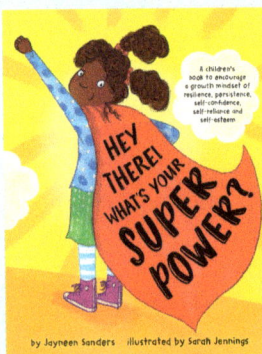

Hey There! What's Your Superpower?

This book provides a number of simple and very achievable 'tasks' to help kids to develop a growth mindset of resilience, persistence, self-confidence, self-reliance and self-esteem. Discussion Questions and extra ideas to boost kids' confidence included. Ages 5 to 11 years

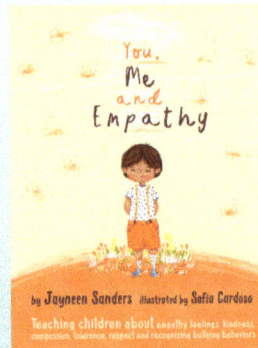

You, Me and Empathy

This charming story uses verse, beautiful illustrations and a little person called Quinn to model the meaning of empathy, kindness and compassion. Discussion Questions and activities to promote empathy and kindness included. Ages 3 to 9 years.

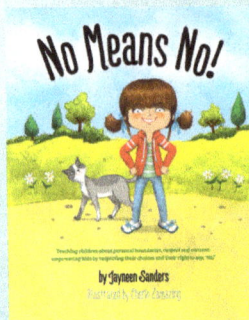

No Means No!

A story about an empowered little girl with a strong voice on all issues, especially those relating to her body! A book to teach children about personal body boundaries, respect and consent. Discussion Questions included. Ages 2 to 9 years.

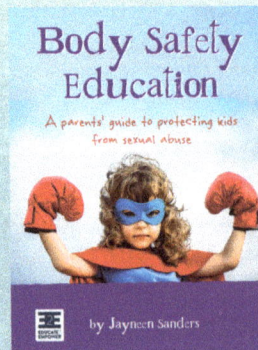

Body Safety Education: A parents' guide to protecting kids from sexual abuse

This essential and easy-to-read guide contains simple, practical, and age-appropriate ideas on how parents, caregivers and educators can protect children from sexual abuse — ensuring they grow up as assertive and confident teenagers and adults.

For more information go to: www.e2epublishing.info